Dreaming on Paper

Waveney Author Group

A message from

Alzheimer's Research UK

All proceeds from this book will go towards Alzheimer's Research UK's pioneering work to find vital treatments and preventions for dementia.

Every copy purchased will bring us one step closer to defeating dementia sooner. We are grateful to all the authors who have written wonderful stories within this book, and to everyone who helped make it possible.

Hilary Evans, Chief Executive at Alzheimer's Research UK, the UK's leading dementia research charity. www.alzheimersresearchuk.org

Copyright © Waveney author group 2016

Published by East Anglian Press

British Library Cataloguing in Publication Data.

A CIP catalogue record for this book is available from the
British Library.
ISBN: 978-0-9954844-2-9

Dreaming on Paper

Waveney Author Group

Contents

Whimsical Writers

The advertisement in the magazine looked intriguing to say the least, it invited people to 'Join a group of Whimsical Writers as they discover the power of the pen on a truly inspirational writing weekend', so here we are. Upon our arrival at the venue, we appear to be the only two here, but we are early, so perhaps the rest will arrive shortly.

After a further ten minutes waiting with no sign of anybody else appearing, Claire and I decide that perhaps we should go in and ask. We enter through the front door and make our way to the reception. We find the desk, but there is still no sign of anybody, the whole place seems utterly deserted. Just then another car pulls up outside, so we wait expecting to be joined by at least one other participant. After a few minutes, a young girl appears and looks quite startled to see us.

'Oh, hello, can I help you? Are you waiting for someone?'

We explain that we are here to join the 'Whimsical Writers', and that we are due to register today at noon. Now her look is one of utter confusion.

'Are you sure that you are in the right place? There have been no bookings here for many months.'

Now it is our turn to look confused.

'What do you mean? We only rang up and booked a week ago. This is The Gossips Hotel and Café is it not?'

The young girl's expression changes again, this time though to one of understanding and almost mild amusement.

'Ah, now I see the confusion, this is indeed The Gossips Hotel, but the café is round the back. There is a group meeting there this weekend, but the hotel is undergoing refurbishment at present. Did you need a room?'

Having travelled nearly ninety miles to get here, we had certainly been expecting a bed for the next two nights.

'Well, yes we are. Are you telling us that there are no rooms available?'

'Oh no, not at all. If you would like to follow me, I will take you round to the café where the rest of the group are gathering. The rooms which you will be staying in are in the cottage attached to the café. Have you driven here today?'

'Yes, our car is parked at the front, do we need to move it?'

'That is up to you, which car is yours?'

This seems a strange question to ask, there are only two out there. Whichever one isn't hers must be ours. But we answer the question anyway.

'Well, the little blue Citroen, why do you ask?'

Her response is our biggest surprise yet.

'So do you happen to know who owns the little black fiesta parked next to you?'

'Well we had assumed it was yours. It wasn't there when we arrived, so no, I'm afraid we can't help you there. We heard it pull up and then you appeared, so we just assumed that you too had just arrived.

'Oh well, no matter, if you would like to follow me now I will take you round to the café, you don't want to be left behind here.'

'What do you mean?'

But she doesn't appear to hear us, and if she does, she does not seem keen to answer. As we follow the girl through the empty hotel, something about this place is making us both feel very uneasy. However, on our arrival at the café any fears of having a wasted journey are soon dispelled, and we are given the warmest of welcomes by the rest of the group.

We turn to thank the girl for her assistance, but she has vanished, she is nowhere to be seen. What is this place we have come to? What is going on here? Well there is one thing for certain; there is no shortage of inspiration! Having been shown to a table, and thoroughly refreshed with some very welcome tea and the most delectable cake, we are finally given the plan for the weekend. There are sixteen of us in total, and this afternoon we are to get into groups of four, find a place in the garden that inspires us, and write about our day so far. Well that sounds easy enough, so Claire and I pair up with the two girls whose table we had been sharing and find our way to a secluded bench seat by a small pond. The tranquility and peace here is almost overwhelming, and the fragrance of cherry blossom hangs in the air, although we fail to see any cherry trees. Nevertheless, we are soon writing away so contentedly that when the time comes for us to return to the café, we forget the time and are late getting back. Not by much, so we don't think anything of it until we enter the café and it is as empty as the hotel had been earlier. Only now there are four of us looking bemused and wondering what on earth is happening.

It is Gillian, one of the other two girls who breaks the eerie silence we now find ourselves in.

'Look, who's that over there? Maybe she can help us?'

As we all turn to look in the direction she is pointing in, Claire and I see the young girl from earlier, only this time something about her seems different. Unable to put our finger on what it is, we decide to ask her for assistance again anyway, but by the time we reach the spot where we had seen her, she has vanished once again.

We now appear to be standing in a walled garden, and just to the left of where we entered is a small wooden door. Assuming that this is how the girl has once again escaped our vision, and hearing merry chatter coming from the other side, we open it. The scene which awaits us is nothing like we had been expecting, it is like a scene straight out of an Austin Novel! What is this place? Have we gone through some sort of time warp? Can these people even see us?

As the four of us stand there staring at each other, the whole image becomes blurry and begins to fade. It is only now that I can feel someone touching my arm and calling my name.

'Sarah, Sarah, you need to get up now. We have to be ready to leave in less than an hour!'

Lazily rubbing sleep from my eyes, I begin to realise that the whole thing had been a dream. Now reality kicks in, I am indeed due to attend a writing weekend beginning today! This could be quite a challenge!

© Helen Thwaites

Something You Have Loved and Lost

Ellie had just answered the telephone to her husband for the tenth time in the last two hours. He had promised he would trust her more. She wasn't fooled by all the excuses he was making. She knew without doubt he was checking up on her, and she was beginning to feel like a prisoner in her own home. As Ellie replaced the receiver she made a decision.

Putting on her thick winter coat and wrapping her favourite scarf around her neck, she started walking. It didn't matter where, she just had to get out of the house. She felt the wind stinging her eyes but didn't care. Forgetting her gloves in her hurry to leave, she pushed her hands down deep into her pockets.

Since moving to Scotland for a fresh start, Ellie was feeling more and more isolated. She had been walking for an hour and realised she was in a part of town unknown to her. Looking up suddenly, she saw a familiar car in the distance coming towards her. Oh no, he was out hunting for her. She darted in the doorway of the building she was passing and slipped inside.

Ten faces looked at her expectantly. Feeling her heart pounding, Ellie was about to apologise for the intrusion when the woman closest to her smiled. 'You look freezing. Come on in and warm yourself up by the fire. You haven't missed much, and the guest author will be here soon.'

'It's time for cake,' a small, kindly looking woman announced. 'Come and sit down and we'll make you a hot drink. I'm Fiona by the way. And you're Elspeth is that right?'

Ellie glanced around at the men and women all sitting around the large table tapping away on their laptops. Checking out the window to make sure her husband's car wasn't lurking there, she sat down by the fire gratefully. 'I'm Ellie' she answered.

'Oh they put the wrong name on the list.'

'Do you write or is this your first time?' a smart elderly gentleman asked. 'It's just that we are always looking for new members on a permanent basis.'

Ellie was amazed at how friendly everyone was and realised that she had inadvertently stumbled on a writers' workshop and she appeared to have been expected.

'Erm, my first time,' she answered, gradually relaxing.

'We don't just write,' the gentleman continued. 'If the weather is good we go for a long walk looking for inspiration.'

'Yes and sometimes we just walk down to the cake shop,' another person said which made all the writers laugh.

Handing Ellie a cup of tea, Fiona sat down next to her. 'Where do you live?'

Ellie gave the address.

'Do you mean to say you've walked all that way? There is a bus you can get,' Fiona added.

Ellie felt uncomfortable. These were the first people that she had really spoken to in the last month and how could she explain? She couldn't tell a bunch of strangers that she was planning a getaway.

'I didn't realise how far it was,' she lied, wondering how on earth she was going to get out of her predicament.

'Hardly anyone new moves to this area. We're so pleased to meet you.'

The others took a break from their writing and gathered round the fire. Ellie realised she was at a community centre. The notice boards displayed the writers weekend with the popular guest author and editor names.

Sipping her tea, Ellie began to feel much better being surrounded by such genuinely kind people. She had been so lonely. She knew Steve was worried about her and she labelled his behaviour as being controlling and possessive.

She was wrong and in denial. She had made a careless comment that had forced him to rush home from work the day before. She was upset and angry that she had lost her baby. It wasn't his fault that the job she had been promised had fallen through. What a mess!

'Are you alright dear?' Ellie realised that everyone was looking at her. Fiona had been asking her something, but she had just been sitting staring blindly ahead. Coming back to earth with a bump Ellie realised that it was up to her. She was being offered friendship, a new interest and the opportunity to be part of a writers group.

'Yes I'm fine, thank you. Can I see what you are working on?'

The woman nearest to the table returned with her laptop and knelt down by Ellie's chair. 'This is our weekend challenge. To write 1,000 words on the subject 'Something you have loved and lost'. I'm writing about my dog.'

Ellie had to blink quickly to hold back the tears. Of all the subjects. The doctor had told her she should write down how she was feeling. This was like an omen.

'I would really like to join your writing group,' Ellie said, surprised at herself, and had to come clean that she hadn't signed up for the writing weekend.

Fiona squeezed her arm as if completely understanding what she was going through.

Although she had been offered a lift home at the end of the day, Ellie preferred to walk as she needed the time to come to terms with everything and decode her emotions. Steve was pacing around as she silently entered the house. One look at his beloved face showed the torment she had put him through.

'You deserve an apology,' Ellie said quickly, before Steve had time to say a word. 'I really am sorry, for what I said yesterday, for going out today and worrying you but I've got some good news.' Steve could tell from his wife's face that something momentous had happened that day.

'I'm going to need a laptop for tomorrow,' she said happily, sharing her news of the writers' weekend that she had encountered and how welcoming everyone had been.

© Rosie Owen

Soaring Heights

"I take my notebook to lunch," said Janet purposefully, on the first day at the Suffolk Country House Writing Forum.

The twelve assorted ladies and gentlemen looked askance at Janet's enthusiasm.

"She knows what she's talking about," whispered Frances to Maisie. "She's probably jotted down snatches of our private conversations!"

"But isn't that what everyone does? Pick up on other people's idle chatter? Sometimes you can get really good ideas for a novel," said Frances encouragingly.

"Like when you're on a bus, if you keep your ears open?"

"Yes. Or wherever there are people: a football stadium, a queue in a bank -"

"- and a masked man bursts in!" - Maisie was getting carried away - "'Stay right where you are, and you'll be fine!'..."

"You'll be fine!" echoed Janet smilingly at the would-be authors. "Now it's elevenses, cake and coffee time!" she announced.

"Cake," mused Frances, "like, you can have your cake and eat it? Or is it that you *can't* have your cake and eat it?"

"It's something I'm addicted to," said Janet. "It's a reward for writing too, and you're going to love writing, AND its rewards."

When everyone had tucked in, Janet continued, "As some of us know each other from previous workshops, we'll start the ball rolling, then the rest of you can say a bit about yourselves. We've all had at least one experience that's worth putting in a story."

Everybody re-arranged themselves attentively.

"Well," began Janet, casting her twinkly eyes around,

"I was awful at English. My teachers kept on about Grammar. I'd dream out of the window and think of my kind grandma and her cat. I was from a large family, but being the eldest girl, I had to get the younger ones ready, soak the washing in a tub, dig up a bucketful of potatoes or cabbages, feed the chickens, and get Grandpa into his special chair, pipe on the wooden table by his side -" At this, two of the ladies agreed knowingly. "All before school. It was the sixties. School dinners were vile -"

"Yes," interrupted one of the sprightly men, "we used to slip horrible mincemeat down into our blazer pockets. Otherwise we were kept back after school and made to eat it." There was a general "Ugh!"

"Anyway," continued Janet, "caring was in my blood, especially for folk in distress. I took to writing to help emotional overload. Gradually I started reading my stories to my clients, who grew to love them. More about this later. Now over to you."

Personal histories unfolded. First Cathy, a quiet girl in red, anxiously looking in her holdall. An only child, cossetted by her parents, she'd never had to lift a finger.

"But I was lonely. Being sent to boarding school was no help. I didn't need a job, so I drifted. My husband was good, in a hunting, shooting, fishing sort of way. I kept a proud house, was adept at entertaining. He died from drink eventually."

"Anxiety dogged her," thought Janet. *"Release her…"*

On through the group. Tom, agile and wiry, was a gardener. Apart from fights with tough boys, he'd left school, bored silly. "I'd never got the hang of reading or writing. Once, I'd been forced to go to Sunday School with my older sister. I was asked to read from the Bible. 'Course, I couldn't. So I scarpered. Never went back. So humiliated I was," he said.

"Another great tale there," said Janet. *"A man of the earth… Pruner of high trees…views, life at the top."*

Frances was next. Originally from New Zealand, she loved English eccentricity, yet now in middle age, was torn. Should she return to the unspoilt landscapes of her childhood, or stay in the grimy London suburbs, in her cheap flat with her faded hippie friends? Janet guessed that Frances was still smitten with jealousy of her sister, only a year younger, who led a successful life in New Zealand, surrounded by antiques. But Frances had taken advantage of so much: *"Education courses, free NHS hips - both!"* Janet was prompted to think. *"Sister rivalry. Ingratitude too. Food there for drama."*

Janet heard everyone. *"In some way,"* she mused, *"they've all been restricted…"*

"Our next exercise is outside," she announced. "You're going to be free. Wander through the grounds, taking in impressions. Jot down anything you see, hear, smell. Be back in half an hour!"

The group stepped through the French windows into the rolling parkland. *"'I love to go a-wandering!'"* hummed Diane, raising a tattooed hand to hitch an imaginary lift, *"'with my knapsack on my back!'"* She linked arms with Tom, who'd bounded up, looking at a neat yew hedge.

"That brings back student memories of hiking round East Germany, before the Wall. Those dark conifers in the Black Forest give me *gothicky* ideas for a ghost tale."

"Forests…yes," said Tom. "And cutting down Brazilian rain-forests. I went out there, you know, to study the tribespeople. Their tales of survival, poachers, and piranhas of the Amazon. I keep meaning to write a thriller about it all."

He was interrupted by a warbling, '*A wandering minstrel, I*,' from Frances and Maisie in chorus.

"That's *The Mikado*," said Maisie. "My Great Aunt Blanche at Cheyne Walk – a real dump then – was seamstress to W. S. Gilbert's wife. *He* used to come occasionally, pacing up and down, while Aunt Blanche was 'fitting.' I could write a comedy about that!"

They listened, smelt, touched, and noted, until the distant chiming of a church clock meant "Time's up!"

Janet greeted them. "Well, you inventive writers? We'll pool your ideas in a minute. First: you all have the chance to come on a tour up North. Our previous group did it. Bronte country. Inspired by the wilderness, reminiscing, gleaning stories from locals. Letting your imagination fly, like a bird…"

"You mean, not *Wuthering Heights,* but *Soaring Heights!*"

© Diana Fernando

Molly's Writing Weekend

Deep breaths. Big smile. 'I can and I will. I can and I will. I can and I -"

Molly didn't see the step until too late and was unable to stop herself falling headlong into the room. Gathering up her scattered books and pens, she pasted on her best 'silly me' grin and dusted off her knees, grateful she had chosen to wear trousers that morning.

"Who put that step there?" Molly's lack of confidence had taken a real nosedive. She had needed a lot of cajoling to get her on this writing weekend, but now she was here. And how!

"Are you OK? Come and get a cuppa," a tall young blonde woman said. "My name's Gill."

"How embarrassing. Only I could have done that," Molly said, gratefully sipping her coffee, careful not to drip any down her top. "I'm Molly."

"If you are ready, shall we get started? For those who haven't met me, I'm Barbara, and I'll begin the introductions."

Molly could feel her neck going red at the mention of having to speak in a group, her mind starting to plan what she could say that would sound remotely interesting. Others were making notes while listening.

'How do they do that?' Molly wondered in awe. She was pleased she hadn't eaten as a rumbling stomach was preferable to seeing her breakfast come up again.

Barbara gave an insight into her background and achievements and passed onto Winnie who spoke freely about her reasons for the autobiography she was planning. The group was enthralled by her words. "I just want to make sure all these memories are not lost forever." Molly was so interested that she almost forgot that her turn was looming.

Vivien was now speaking. Molly was next. Her stomach flipped. But her turn took a while to come round as Vivien could talk. Oh, how she could talk! She was interesting, but all Molly wanted was for her turn to be over. 'How on earth do I follow that?'

"And now over to Molly."

"Sorry, I'm not used to this," she apologised. But after a faltering start she surprised herself and was pleased that they all appeared interested as she finished.

Passing the virtual baton to her neighbour Stella, she was able to relax and enjoy the experiences that were being shared. There were seven participants, from all walks of life; even a titled lady who assured them she didn't like to use it. She was Charlotte, but preferred Charly with a Y. "I hate being called Lady, I'd rather get down and dirty with whatever's going on," she said with a grin. Molly really warmed to Charly.

Barbara set the first task of the day. Thirty words to write about your favourite cake. Wow, where to start. Lemon drizzle, carrot cake, doughnuts. Settling for chocolate brownie, Molly started in earnest and found herself salivating as she wrote. Dark, moist, sweet. Hot or cold. Shall I have it with cream? Mmm, how long until lunch break?

Believe it or not there were no duplicate cake stories.

Stella had cup-cakes. She looked like a cup cake kind of girl. Gill was a cream horn. Elegant and well turned. Charly was black forest gateaux. No surprise there.

Surprisingly Vivien was the simple mince pie. And so they went on.

By the time they stopped for a break Molly felt quite at home within the group. The cake exercise had been a real icebreaker and Molly was surprised how she easily she mingled.

"I loved your take on chocolate brownie. I could almost taste it," said Barry. Molly had thought him quite boring as he was so into technology, something that Molly disliked intensely. It scared her.

"Yours sounded tasty too," answered Molly, blushing as she realised how this might have sounded. But Barry thanked her, oblivious to her embarrassment.

Barry told her he lived about an hour away. "My wife booked this course as a gift for me. She thinks I have a talent; but I'm not sure. I enjoy playing with words though."

"Me too. My Dad always said 'Molly you'll get your nose stuck in that book' but I get lost in them."

"Have you seen Joan's sketches?" Barry asked. "She's putting them in the kiddies' books she's writing. They're amazing."

Joan appeared to be an austere lady but she was quite the opposite. She turned out to be so charismatic and had the most amazing imagination. They were all in stitches listening to her tales. Molly was surprised at how her usual good instinct had misjudged both Barry and Joan.

She was intrigued by John though. He had an unkempt exterior with blond dreadlocks, casual colourful clothing and appeared a little 'way out, man'. He was different, the sort Molly would not normally associate with. She noticed immediately that he had the most beautiful deep blue eyes. His genre of writing was poetry; beautiful, sensitive poetry.

He and Barry appeared so different but she noticed them deep in conversation and laughing together.

"See you all tomorrow,' Barbara said, bringing the first day to a close.

"Mind the step today," John said with a chuckle to Molly as they met in the car park on day two.

"Don't remind me," she grinned.

"Today's first exercise is to split into pairs, talk to each other for 5 minutes each and write about what you learned," Barbara instructed.

Molly was paired with Vivien. "Vivien isn't at all as I assumed," Molly fed back. "My first impressions were that she likes to talk but actually she told me she is one of eight children and has had to work hard to be heard. She has a beautiful soul and that really came through. I'm glad we had the chance to talk."

"Well, Molly should not hide away. She puts herself down but she shouldn't. She has a wealth of knowledge and a very empathetic nature."

Molly felt herself grow in stature.

Listening to the rest of the groups feedback she felt inspired and grateful to have been a part of this writing weekend.

It had been a valuable, cathartic experience for Molly and she walked tall over the step as she left for home.

© Patricia Casselden

Fighting, Biting and Writing

As Sammy snake slipped out of his old skin, he felt reborn, slinky, unrestricted and ready to slither into this delicious day. Meanwhile Catrina cat was busy doing her exercises, s-t-r-e-t-c-h-i-n-g like an Octupus. She let out a mighty yawn which bordered on being a little catastrophic. Oh good, salmon biscuits and fresh water. My owner has proved to be a good slave to me. Catrina had time to languish, she licked her coat, paying special attention to her ears. Just a little catnip and a nap, then I'm off, she thought, purrfect.

Dougie the dog was straining at the leash, as he wanted his owner to hurry up over the Zebra crossing, while everyone was saying Hyena, how are you, ducky? Later, when the lead was removed, he wolfed his food rather unceremoniously. Dougie then felt a little horse, so his owner, Ena, gave him a drink before hugging him and said, "Now be a little dear and I'll see you after work, along with lizard, alligator and donkey. Joey will hop over and feed you later."

Dougie loved home, but couldn't wait to meet up with his friends. Pretty soon, Sammy snake, Catrina cat and Dougie dog were talking together. They had been joined by Bert bird, Ellie elephant, Len lion and Shelly tortoise, plus Charlie chimp.

Positioned in her usual authorised place was the leader of their group, the very foxy colourful Ursula Fairy-Dust unicorn. They all greeted each other and chatted about their various beefs, offals and joys. Everyone adored Sammy's new skin. "It suits you, takes years off your age, the crocodile-skin look has gone, along with the turkey neck," remarked Ellie elephant.

Ursula Fairy-Dust said, "OK, let's get underway. At our last session you were given the prompt of humans!" The animals sat listening to each other's prose, they were all quiet as mice, then they each commented. For some reason, perhaps the weather, which had become overcast, there was an air of discontent. Bert, being a little gullible and acting somewhat like a lady-bird, made Catrina really fed up, so she ate him. Hissing off Sammy snake thought Charlie chimp's apeing about was making a monkey out of everyone, so Sammy decided to cuddle him very tightly and soon Charlie chimp met his demise.

Sammy glided away a little sheepishly. Being a snake which had a reputation for a night on the tiles, he was more than rattled and wound up about an upcoming stag do. "I must learn to unwind," he thought. A flea landed on Dougie, which got his goat, and he started running around gnashing shark-like teeth. Dougie ended up chasing Catrina out of the meeting. They found themselves out in the cold where it was raining the proverbial cats and dogs. Both were dog tired, they realised that they had been a trifle catty about some things. They would be glad when the weather turned a little 'otter.

The other members were beeing, and feeling, ratty, rabbiting away about antisocial behaviour, how cowardly some were, perhaps? "If this wasn't so horrible we could have a right giraffe," said Ellie elephant. Shelly tortoise had retreated into her very own mobile home.

It was agreed to hedge, not to hog, their written words, preventing the remaining book-worm friends from slugging things out when they felt so crabby or fishy and nobody would be toads or swanning about. No more feathers or hares to be ruffled, nor getting under anyone's skin.

Hopefully the writers' group wouldn't be so chicken-hearted and fowl-mouthed. Perhaps they could stop acting like wildebeests. Len, who was a dandy lion, lost his pride, manely because of hunger. Longing for some chocolate moose, he stormed off in a rage, and rammed Shelly tortoise underfoot. She was now the size of a snail, and squealed "owl!" So that sealed her fate, the world was not her oyster after all.

Ellie elephant said "tusk tusk," as she politely collected her writing materials, not forgetting her sister's pen and Camella's books, packing them into her mammoth trunk before heading back to their mother. Ursula Fairy-Dust unicorn was left feeling devoid of colour, like a rhinestone-less rhino, but then the sun came out and so did her sparkle. She thought, "I will conjure up some genteel mythical creatures for the new authors' circle, and the prompt will be unicorns in Unison.

Time flew by, as Ursula Fairy-Dust was still learning about her magical powers. She gazed upon the new gathering presented to her. She was aghast and fearfully thought her horn would surely drop off, because she was greeted by a herd of purple swine that were trotting nervously near her, as they felt penned in.

After her initial shock, she decided, "Well, as long as they don't tell too many porkies, we can ham it up without anyone becoming a silly sausage, or getting the chop. Who knows, these pigs may sprout wings, and we can all fly. Also, I will learn not to muck up my spells in future, otherwise they could all become a load of old bull."

Composing herself, Ursula tuned into her horn, making a cornucopia of gifts. She was able to magic up some guineas and bucks, hoping to badger rich, not poultry folk, into providing new posh venues for the Writers' Weekends. Now we will all bear up, no one should get the butterflies either, so we will be happy bunnies at last, and, just maybe, us writers will have a whale of a time.

My nightmare tail could drag-on, but I do not want to boar you so I'm frog marching off to Henley to see one's slightly old fashioned out-dated friend, T rex. He'll warm the cockles of my hart. He's my Mr mussels. We are going to the hippodrome for some honest fun, no cheetahs allowed!

© Karen J A Nunn

What a Mistake to Make

The sun has just pierced the leaden sky. Can this be April? Surely not! I hope the group I am about to join will be warmer and more friendly than this grim, grey, hail-punctuated day. The lazy North-easterly wind is determined to hold me back from reaching my destination. My freezing, exposed hands are clinging to both my book and my walking stick, at least the flowers have remembered to bloom! Rows of daffodils nod and sway while primroses peep through the grasses. I battle on regardless and cope determinedly with the steps. At last, the thought of warmth relaxes me as I mount the steps of this very impressive building. Busy and bustling, everyone seems to know where to go and what to do - at high speed. Me, I'm still trying to negotiate those steps!

At last I make it to the entrance, where I enjoy the warmth and busy chatter. What will this new group be like? Every other group has been friendly and encouraging. I am bound to find some different people today. We have been warned that some people can be jealous and mean, while others will pretend to be friends but turn out to be anything but!

Now to remember the way, with a deep breath I enter the room. A familiar place where I have made many friends, but this time I am uncertain. Even the furniture has been changed. Everyone in the room looks very young, and far more confident than I have ever been. Unusually for a writing group, there is a majority of young men. A powerful, yet intelligent looking bunch, they seem more suitable to appear on a rugby field than in a writing group! The girls appear to be very pleased with themselves, immaculate make-up and 'with it' clothes, whose long painted nails proclaim no washing-up in the last year, and how do they use their computers?

I take my place on the girls' side, feeling decidedly out of place. The chat in the room fades, and I suddenly feel the eyes of men and girls staring at me. I shuffle uncomfortably. My stick clatters onto the floor, followed by my notebook and pen. This cannot be my new group! I smile and whisper, "Hello." Nobody speaks or smiles back at me. It is enormously embarrassing!

Eventually I cannot bear the silence any longer. I leave the room and stand outside, uncertain about what to do next. A young man appears carrying many name tags on ribbons. I do not need a name tag, having attended enough of these courses to know the form. Instead, we write our name on a piece of paper, and put the paper on the table in front of us, big enough for all to see, even without appropriate glasses. This is not the meeting I was hoping for. Hot, and red with embarrassment, I make my way back to reception and ask about the 'Get Writing' workshops.

'The writing weekend is next week dear.' This explanation comes from the kindly and patient receptionist on duty. I had obviously tried to join the entertainment staff!

© Enid Thwaites

"...and the Winner is..."

Stella Starburst nodded 'Good light years' to her task-robot, stepped from her work terminus and iris-ed the exit lock. The panel slid away and she transported herself to the CreativeCypherPod. Once docked, Stella murmured a greeting to everyone and chose a couch next to a lexical station.

Nina Nebula said, 'Okay. We're all here, so we'll push on and it's all good news. Firstly, about the *InterCosmicFestival* - our shuttle has been chosen to host it.' Nina paused to let the news be absorbed, then continued, 'I am over the moon at the prospect of us being able to showcase our writing and to date we have confirmation of fifty humanoids from four of the inner galaxies, six from the outer ones attending, and there has been a tentative query from the androids on Galaxy M100.'

'Wow,' Tom Telluric punched his fists in the air.

A ripple of satisfied whispering ran around the pod.

'But before we discuss the somnolence arrangements and sustenance preferences for all the visitors I think we should take a short break.'

The group looked puzzled. Nina laughed. 'Then…I will announce…the winner of…the Writing Competition.'

Once in the White Dwarf Bar, it was drinks all round. Stella had downed two welkins and tonics before most of her colleagues had had a chance to palm their order at the pump automaton. She gulped down another one; the Bar was getting rowdy.

After two more welkins, Stella tossed all the little blue paper umbrellas into the suction tidy, pulled her leggings into a better shape, re-buttoned her epaulettes, and made her way along the pedestrian tube. She was so nervous, and knew that in 18% more digital time, she would find out how successful she had been in the writing competition.

She had worked really hard on the story – the amount of research she'd undertaken would have exhausted the most intellectual alien. Then the imbibe button on her belt began flashing a warning orange. Stella stopped at the Recuperative Hub; she first put her head in the Detox Box and took several deep breaths, then stood in front of the Optical Illusion Wall and pressed the "Complete Redo Spray" button for her face, neck and hair.

Back in the CreativeCyberPod the air was nucleonic with excitement. Nina touched the wall screen and shafts of green, blue, red, intermingled and formed the words

IntergalaticWritingWeekend
The Winning Entry

Stella felt a tightening in her throat and pulled at the collar of her tunic.

Nina spoke. 'The winner of this competition will be reading their work at the *InterCosmicFestival*...'

'Wow,' Tom Telluric punched his fists in the air.

'Thank you Tom.' Nina touched the screen again and the letters skimmed, flittered, reformed, to read

IS...

Nina went on, 'and also *Orbit Cloud* will broadcast it on the asteroid station: frequency 58.000.'

Stella looked away from the screen and fidgeted with the clips on her left boot.

'So,' continued Nina, 'before we know who the winner is, let me also say that the winning story will be created as an Entertainment Disk and will be available at the *InterCosmicFestival*.'

No one spoke. Nina turned to Tom.

'Wow,' Tom Telluric punched his fists in the air.

'Thank you Tom.'

Because everyone was looking at each other and laughing, Stella had a moment to herself after she read her name on the screen before the room vibrated to a unison of 'Wows!' Then all the other writers switched on their communicating buttons, highlighted the "thumbs up" icon and shone them towards her.

Nina beckoned Stella to come and stand by the Narrator Dais.

'Would you like to give us a little idea of what your story is about Stella?' asked Nina.

'Yeah, give us the blurb,' called out Anni Altazimuth."

'Well,' smiled Stella, 'The story is set aeons ago; sort of in the days of paper and pens, you know.'

'Bor-ing,' muttered Anni.

'Ssshhh,' Nina made the sound seem like the disconnecting of an air siphon.

'U-m-m, and laptops, of course, and it's about a group of writers like us, but the main part of the story is …' Stella paused and looked across at Karrel Krator who was skimming her personal data pad.

'Yes,' Stella said, 'It is really about the social side of communicating in those long ago days and the story is called "A Pot of Tea and a Piece of Cake".'

Karrel Krator looked up, 'A pot of what?' she asked. Stella Starburst shook her head, chuckled and sat down.

© Pam Finch

Weekend of Promise

'Come on, we'll be late,' Sarah shouted as she hurried down the stairs. John came running behind her doing up his shirt, socks hanging over his shoulder. He would just about make it outside of the door dressed. Sarah got to the car first and jumping into the driver's seat she revved the engine, her agitation very clear in her actions.

'We need to get a shift on, John. It's an hour away to the hotel and we have to book in by ten o'clock!'

'Alright, alright,' he answered back, as he jumped into the passenger's seat only to realise he had left his briefcase. Sarah's tolerance levels were slipping completely by the time he got back and his apologies fell on deaf ears.

They drove in silence, both wondering if it might have been better to have stayed at home. If he hadn't come over so early enticing her into bed they would be well on their way by now. At last, the signpost showing they only had four miles to go. Their hotel was in the centre of the small market town of Beccles, so shouldn't be too hard to find.

Drawing up into the car park, they gathered their bags and hurried to reception with minutes to spare. It was going to be a good weekend and the writing course would be something to talk about when they got home...it was so good to be somewhere where nobody would know them. They had decided to stay two nights at the hotel and celebrate their anniversary; it was three years tomorrow since they had met.

Sarah had moved in four doors from John and from the first time they met there was an attraction to each other. She would watch in the mornings as he passed by to go to work and as time went on he would wave to her as he went by.

'I'm sorry,' she said, hugging him. 'Let's not argue, we have waited so long for this, he kissed her head gently taking in the fragrance of her perfume. They chucked their bags into their room and hurried down to the writing group. Tables and chairs were already set up for the group and apart from a young disheveled man who probably came straight from a night out with the lads, a pretty blonde girl about the same age and a man with a rather large moustache already busy on his laptop, they were the only ones there.

They sat down next to the young man and introduced themselves. He smiled not offering any information back. The room began to fill up, amongst them a lady who looked like an old school teacher she once had, same build same way of walking. She sank down into her seat hoping she was wrong. It was hard to tell, so many years had passed. She had told friends and family the writing group was much further away than it was. All it needed was one person, and the whole town where she lived would know where she had been.

The last time she went away for a spa weekend to celebrate her mums sixtieth, they turned up full of alcohol and good cheer and her mother never forgave them or her. She looked at John and smiled, he looked out of his depth among all the laptops paper and pens. He only agreed to come so they could be together. A chance to decide their future together, they both knew they couldn't go on like this forever, never committing to one another. But for now they just wanted to enjoy this time together.

The lady taking the course this morning was very confident in her subject, making it seem like anything was possible. She set them a task to write a short story of 250 words on the topic, "Why are you here this weekend?" Already the task lay before her like a ravine she would have to jump to finish. She could answer that in four words. "To be with John," but she decided on "To be with people who enjoyed writing as much as she did, and to learn as much as she could to help her become a published author." This was also true.

They broke for lunch at midday and decided to go for a stroll around the town, stopping at a small cafe where they chatted about the group and about their plans for the weekend. The afternoon session was on self-publishing and discussing what they wanted from the weekend. Everyone was friendly and they got to know some of the group better by the end of the session. They had dinner the evening in the hotel, and spent the night in each other's arms, pent up emotions pouring out in their desire for each other. John woke up early, and kissing Sarah, he jumped out of bed to shower.

As he stood under the warm running water he thought about the day ahead, slightly daunted by the prospect. He found the writing course difficult, he wasn't a writer and his effort at 250 words was just waffle. He thought about the evening ahead, his plans for their anniversary. Dinner at a posh restaurant, flowers, and a ring, although he wondered if the ring was maybe going a bit too far.

The rest of the day was much like the day before, today was more about publicity, a bit more up John's street, and he felt he got more involved than he had yesterday. At the end of the day they said their goodbyes, swapping phone numbers with people they had got to know including the disheveled young man who it turned out was named Kevin and was a teacher in the local high school. Who would have thought?

Certainly not John, he had him down as a musician in a group playing heavy metal. It turned out that the lady Sarah was so worried out wasn't her old teacher, and was in fact the owner of a B&B not far away.

Walking back to their room they linked arms and smiled at each other looking forward to the evening ahead. The restaurant was just down the street so they strolled together in the soft evening light. The food was amazing, the flowers beautiful, and the ring...a promise of a future together. The emotion of the evening stayed with them as they walked back to their hotel. Going to their room, they went straight to bed with thoughts of tomorrow and going home bringing down their happiness. They fell asleep entwined in each other's arms.

Too soon the morning came, they packed and headed downstairs to check out, then headed for the double doors leading to the car park. In the distance they spotted a couple obviously very much in love, arms around each other, they kissed a long drawn out kiss, another couple here to spend time together alone. As they came closer, Sarah's eyes opened wide in shock and she tried to steer John away but too late. They came face to face with Sarah's husband, and John's wife…

© Shirley Newstead

Who killed Quentin Barbary?

Lucille

Lucille looked at him and thought she hated her husband. Although hate is such a strong word and she had never before allowed herself to use it. He was coming through the kitchen door now, tapping away with his stick.

'Where are you, woman? Make yourself known.'

She hated him calling her 'woman'. She hated his loud, tetchy voice. She had stopped telling him about all the things she objected to because he never listened – he just spoke over her as if she hadn't uttered a word.

They got married ten years ago in a fit of passion. Quentin Barbary was a soldier, tall, broad, athletic. Lucille's love for him was all consuming. She knew that he was starting to lose his sight. But, because she imagined him heroic, she thought he would gradually lose his sight in a heroic fashion. He didn't.

He liked being looked after and from depending on his wife he transformed into a demanding, complaining despot. He grew fat while his wife grew thinner. Lucille stayed with him out of duty and pity.

They both belonged to a local writing group and this weekend had booked onto the group's annual Writing Weekend. It was always set in a scenic part of the country in a remote location. The members had formed quite close friendships.

Lucille was contemplating murder. She always did the right thing and in her state of mind murder was the right thing. She knew that within the group Quentin was more loathed than tolerated. There were a number of their friends who would have reason to do away with him and this would provide her cover.

Philippa

Philippa was the writing group organiser. Quiet and determined, she spoke few words because she carefully selected her words for good expression. Not so Quentin Barbary! His presence was always loudly declared and his superiority assumed. He dominated any gathering and preached to them on all subjects, literary or not. Philippa was still seething from his contribution the last time they all met.

'Of course we don't have a leader of sorts for this group. Leadership is nurtured in the military, don't you know! And the writing standard of this group can only be as high as that of its members. With one or two exceptions this group turns out utter drivel!'

Her writing group only went well if he was absent. In fact, most members had stopped writing.

Both Quentin and Lucille were coming to the Writing Weekend. This year she had booked a room in an olde worlde pub nestled deep in the southern hills. Philippa had a plan. To restore sanity and creativity to her group. It involved murder.

Gideon

Gideon Goodchild was a mild mannered man. His writing group companions found him polite and gracious. Everyone knew he kept a pit bull terrier, named Brute, muzzled but manic. Some thought this surprising as a dog usually assimilates the traits of its master. Really vicious dogs are trained to attack – but that wouldn't be the case with Gideon, would it?

Gideon was a wronged man. He loved his wife, Julia, but strongly suspected that her affections had removed themselves to another man. To be precise, to Quentin Barbary. Julia had never read a book in her life and found her husband's literary interests boring and time wasting. She had formed an alliance with the odious Quentin because it amused her to hear him berate the stupid pen pushers. In Gideon's mind, and only in his mind, they had become flagrant lovers.

Gideon had noticed that the colour red set off a tic in Brute. Left to his own devices, Brute would attack a red object. Gideon therefore trained Brute in not just attacking but to apply all his viciousness and to devour a red object until only the crumbs were left.

Yes, Gideon would go to the Writing Weekend, with Brute.

The Writing Weekend

Philippa intended the group members to 'get in touch with their inner voice' whilst on the writing weekend. They were to make the most of the unspoilt countryside and in this most calming setting write a piece coming straight from that inner voice. On Sunday afternoon they were all to share their writing.

In the pub the group sessions were to be held in the snug, which was situated above the beer cellar. The barman had shown Philippa where to sit to be in easy reach of the flip switch that opened the trapdoor. 'You can get rid of anyone you don't like. As they walk across it flip the switch and down they go!' he joked.

Gideon phoned Quentin a few days before the event with the pretence of mulling over this theme – our inner voice. He endured Quentin's verbal abuse for a full ten minutes before ending the conversation with 'By the way, Julia says you look good in red.'

Lucille drove to the pub location with Quentin as passenger. He had the maddening habit of sticking out his arms in the direction he thought they should take, shrieking 'Right', 'Left'. At the last right turn he had smacked Lucille in the face and she was sporting a swollen eye which was turning purple.

Lucille, a one-time chemistry teacher, had a small phial of concentrated, distilled apricot kernels – cyanide, in her handbag. She was waiting for Sunday afternoon.

Friday evening and all through Saturday the group took walks, everyone taking turns to support and guide

Quentin. At the point when they all should have been inspired, Sunday afternoon commenced. They were to have tea at about two o'clock. Lucille offered to prepare it and gave everyone their cups. With her back turned she slipped the cyanide into Quentin's cup and put it on the occasional table next to him.

Quentin had worn a dusky pink shirt on Friday. On Saturday it had been a deep fuchsia. Today it was bull's blood red.

Gideon sat by the door with Brute, leashed, beside him. Quentin was pontificating about the difference between the gerund and the present participle. He wasn't getting much response from the group so, gesticulating, he rose to his feet and stomped forward. Gideon unleashed Brute.

Philippa flipped the switch just as Quentin's foot hovered above the trapdoor. The red apparition shot down the hole. Brute flew through the air howling and crashed into the occasional table sending the tea up into the air and the cup smashed against the ceiling.

Down in the cellar Quentin sat on a mattress, stunned. Intuitive staff had placed a mattress below the hole to lessen the impact of drunken pranks.

Now Quentin had enough self-knowledge to perceive that he was hated. Up he got from the mattress and made his way, banging and tapping on the walls, to the snug. All the writers sat staring at the hole (Brute too, leashed again). Quentin made his entrance at the door.

'My fellow writers' he boomed, rubbing his hands together in glee, 'What have your inner voices been telling you? The same old utter drivel I expect!'

No-one said a word and no-one had written a word.

© Helen Meneghello

Dream On

"But they're all women," I complained, scanning the list of participants for the writing weekend I'd signed up for. "I'm doing this to meet people, and by people, I mean men."

Lizzie, my best friend, sighed. "Is that all you think about?" she asked. "Men?"

"No, not all," I said, patiently, "but I would like to meet someone nice, and I thought a writer's weekend might have potential. I don't want to meet a bloke in the pub, because I'm not looking for a bloke who goes to the pub all the time, I want one with a bit more about him."

I'd better explain before I start sounding desperate. I was widowed ten years ago, my children are grown up, and I'd like some uncomplicated male company. I've got a lot of great female friends and we share a lot. But I do miss having a man about the place. Not just to put out the bins and retrieve spiders from the bath, but for another point of view, and let's face it, the sex. I'm not getting any younger and I want to make the most of whatever energy I've got left.

Although I was looking forward to the writing weekend, it was a bit disappointing that we were all women. I had hopes of meeting someone intelligent and articulate. I dreamed of philosophical conversations, long into the night, in front of an open fire. Walks on the beach, maybe with a couple of photogenic dogs, discussing politics and current affairs. Picnics, pub lunches, drives through the countryside, weekends in London seeing plays and exhibitions.

I don't know who I was kidding, really. I'd been happily married for twenty years and we'd never had a philosophical conversation. The only art in the house was stuck on the fridge and dated back to the kids' schooldays. And despite living a spit from the beach, I got down there about three times a year when I felt guilty about the dogs' quick twice-a-day drag round the block, and bundled them off for a proper walk, after which they both fell into a deep and resentful sleep.

Lizzie thought I was barking up the wrong tree. "If there were any men on your course they'd probably be sensitive artistic types." She shuddered. "Ugh. They'd want to talk about their feelings all the time. Come on, let's go down to the King's Head. You might not meet Mr Right, but we can have a glass of wine and do the quiz."

"Hello, laydeez," leered Al, the lecherous landlord, leering myopically at Lizzy's cleavage. She rearranged her scarf. "Hi Al, two large reds, please."

There was a table in the corner, so I grabbed it while Lizzie paid for the round. Quiz nights usually got busy, and I didn't fancy having to stand at the bar fending off Amorous Al, although I don't think it was me he was keen on. He would flirt with anyone though, just to keep his hand in.

Lizzie came back to the table with our drinks, looking sheepish. She was followed by a tall, sandy haired man with a pint of beer and an apologetic expression.

"This is Bob," Lizzie said to me. "He's just moved here and doesn't know anybody. Till now. Bob, this is Anita. I've asked Bob to join us for the quiz," she continued.

"Do you know anything about sport?" I asked him. I'm very competitive about the pub quiz, and he was welcome to join us if he could fill the gaps in our collective knowledge.

"A bit," he told me. "But it's not really my subject. Thanks for letting me join you. I was getting a bit sick of the landlord's jokes." Since Al's jokes had all come out of a cracker in about 1953, it didn't take long to get bored with them.

Bob was easy to get on with and we won the quiz, despite him knowing nothing about sport. He fielded one or two tricky questions, though, one about Aristotle that went right over my head, and another one about something I'd missed on the news last week.

Once or twice I thought he seemed to be looking at me speculatively. You know, *that* look, the one that men get when they might be a bit interested, and they are wondering whether to chance their arm or not. But, as I kept telling Lizzie, I wasn't after a man who spends all his spare time in the pub, so as far as Bob was concerned, I was out of bounds.

"What do you do?" Lizzie asked him, in a break between questions. "I'm more or less retired," he told us. "I moved here because I always fancied living near the sea, and I've some family nearby. I'm looking forward to walking my dogs on the beach."

Lizzie nudged me. I stood on her foot under the table, just in case she got any ideas about matchmaking. He might have been a nice bloke, and he wasn't bad looking, but I wasn't going to break my bloke-in-the-pub rule for anybody. Besides, I had my writing weekend coming up and didn't need any complications just then.

Life got busy for a week or two. I visited my daughter, who was desperate for me to meet someone. "I hate to think of you on your own," she said. "I wish you'd meet somebody nice. I'm sure dad wouldn't mind."

"It's not that," I reassured her. "I just haven't met anyone. I never go anywhere, and I signed up for the Get Writing weekend hoping there might be someone, but they're all women."

"Oh well," she said, "I'm sure you'll enjoy yourself anyway."

I wasn't sure about anything. I'd signed up on a whim and I'd never written anything in my life. Still, I fancied having a go, so despite the initial disappointment at the lack of male participants, I set off optimistically with my shiny new notebook and pen, like a kid off to school. I had thought about buying a pencil case, but I never like to look too keen.

When I arrived at the hall, there was already quite a crowd gathered. Altogether there were fifteen of us, aged from 27 to knocking on for 80, fat, thin and most points in between, blonde, brunette, grey and, startlingly, pink. But all female. They all seemed lovely, but definitely all female.

One of the women, an enthusiastic sixty-something in yoga trousers and a hideous mahogany perm, had apparently been on one of these weekends before. She was disappointed, she said. "The usual tutor is off sick, and they've had to get a replacement. It's a shame. Poppy is so lovely. I hope she's ok."

I'd never met Poppy, so I didn't mind, but I did wonder who they would get to replace her at such short notice. We talked among ourselves for a while, then there was a cough from the front of the room where our new tutor was waiting patiently for us to quieten down. Blondish, tall and familiar.

"Good morning, ladies," he said, looking at us each in turn. I don't know whether I imagined it, but I'm sure he winked at me. "I'm retired really, but I've stepped in to help out since Poppy is ill. My name is Bob."

© Jo Wilde

Oh George!

It's been a busy day cleaning the house, I didn't like doing it at the start but once into it, it was okay. Of course, I have been doing more than just housework, oh yes, I've been busy keeping my social networking sites up to date. Facebook took the longest, so many posts to read and respond too, oh, and of course there are the stupid ones where people post a photo of what they're having to eat.

Peter is meeting a friend for a meal after work so I throw a spag bol in the microwave, and after eating it I sit down with a cuppa and cake. I'm still sat there an hour later when I hear the key in the door. Peter's home. I look to the door and smile as he comes through it. Eating again, are we? his eyes say.

I cheerfully say 'Hi darling, busy day?' Not that I care but it's polite to ask, isn't it? 'Oops!' I say as I bite into the cream slice and the cream squirts out and drops onto my lap. I want to scoop it up with my index finger but perfect Peter has arrived with a piece of kitchen roll.

We've been living together for eight months and I feel there are times when he still doesn't get me, especially when I am writing and staring into space as he calls it. I tell him I'm thinking, and he smiles. He takes his jacket off and hangs it on the back of the chair. He will take it upstairs when he goes up. How do I know? It happens every night after he's been to work.

Peter has been working so hard at the library since the council decided to sell it and the long hours mean we hardly spend any time together which is fine really as I get time to make up stories, I hadn't planned to do anything with them, just keep them safe in my exercise book, but when Bernie rings asking if I want to go to a writing weekend on Saturday I jump at the chance and reply with a big yes!

Half an hour later I am sat with my laptop in the dining room, oh, and a bottle of wine, well not a bottle exactly, well yes it is a bottle but it's not a full bottle. Where was I? Oh yes, so I'm sat with my laptop googling the writing workshop. I pour the wine and take a sip. Mmm. I lick my lips and think about the writing weekend. Who will be there? Will they all be published authors?

I start to get a little nervous and it doesn't help when Bernie sends me an email:

From: Bernie@iloveshopping&moreshopping.co.uk
To:　Erica@ilovecake&morecake.co.uk

Hi Erica,
Feeling rough won't be able to make the writing weekend.
Soz
Bernie x

I take a gulp of wine, pull my exercise book from my bag and read through some of my stories.

***

I look around the room and everyone bar one has a laptop opened in front of them. One person has an A4 writing pad and two pens and I decide to sit next to her, mainly because I have a pad and two pens too.

'Can I get you a drink? Tea? Coffee?' proffered a George Clooney lookalike.

'Um, oh, um,' I spluttered. 'Toffee, please.'

'Toffee?' he questioned, with a cheeky smile that made me blush.

I tried to clear my throat but the word 'tea' still came out croaky. He smiled and came back with my tea. My face reddened even more, in fact I think it must have been the colour of beetroot. I watched him walk to the front of the room.

Trying to stop fantasising about 'George' wasn't easy, and I didn't hear a thing about Getting Started and Planning your writing, nor Editing or How to Write a Synopsis, but I did hear when he said he would put his contact information up on the screen, and turned and did so.

Not wishing to be obvious, I looked at the other writers to see who was copying his details. Only a few. I slowly wrote down his number, trying not to show how much I wanted it. I listened to him tell us about the different styles of publishing, and how easy it is to independently publish a book.

Lunch was great, not only good tasty food, but it gave us writers time to mingle and chat. Surprising how many were nervous, and at the same time as excited about their writing as I was. No one mentioned 'George'.

The afternoon involved an exercise walking through the grounds along the fishing lake, and writing down what we saw and how we felt. 'George' said to remember all five senses, hearing, taste, seeing, smell and touch. Oooh, how I would like to touch. 'No, stop it, come on,' I tell myself, 'do the exercise and concentrate.'

Four o'clock comes and I am looking forward to going home and writing up today's exercise. I am buzzing! I walk with two of the writers, Dorothy and Monica, to the car park. I look to the lake on our left and ask, 'Is that a lake or is it a pond?'

Monica turns to look, 'Not big enough for a lake.'
'Or deep enough,' Dorothy chips in.
'For what?' I ask.
'To drown him,' they say in unison, and the three of us laugh.

No words are exchanged as we walk to our cars, apart from 'See you tomorrow,' as we open the car doors.

***

Noticing Peter's car on the gravelled drive, I quickly turn the key in the door, all excited to tell him about my writing day and the drowning in the pond, or is it a lake? Anyway, where was I? Oh yes, so I rush into the lounge and am stopped in my tracks by Peter.

He's stood up holding a box with a bow on it. He proffers the box, and I quickly untie the lilac ribbon, so thoughtful, lilac is my favourite colour. I open the box and it's filled with note pads, pens and, of course, cake. Lowering the box to the table I hug Peter and whisper, 'Thank you.'

'Get writing and publish those stories. I will be honoured to have your work, in book form, on one of my shelves.'
'Really?'
'Yes, now go and stare into space.'

***

On the second day some of us volunteer to share our thoughts of the first day and how it has helped us to shape our writing and given us the confidence to carry on writing.

George says, 'You don't need to be good at editing, you can pay people to do that, just be a good writer and let the editors edit and the book designers create your covers.' Wise words from a wise, and gorgeous, man. I think to myself.

'I know what I'm going to do,' says Monica, and we all look at her. 'This weekend has really motivated me and I'm going to write and publish a book.' We all chorused, 'Me too!' and the group united. We are buzzing! And the buzz takes us to the café for refreshments as we talk about how we will do it, and how we will meet once a month to support each other. I hope we do meet.

© Suzan Collins

About the Authors

Karen JA Nunn

I was hatched in Essex but now nest in Suffolk. My family tree is growing, as I am soon to become a grandmother again. I write partly because I want to leave a legacy for these darling grandchildren. Belonging to a writers' group in Suffolk I feel has enabled me to burst out of my bud, and blossom with my writing skills. I certainly have caught the writer's bug in many genres. At this moment in time I have two runner up places in short story competitions under my wings. I hope to be included in a writer's booklet soon as well.

I am more than thrilled to have been asked to write a part of this wonderful, worthy book. In fact I am as proud as a Suffolk Punch to be involved with this particular charitable cause.

Pat Casselden

Pat writes under the pen name of Tricia Cass and enjoys writing humorous poetry and short stories. No Going Back is her debut novel.

https://www.facebook.com/Tricia-Cass-Author-100423340370911/?fref=ts

Helen Meneghello

Helen has a non-fiction book published and is working on a children's book – all about bees. Helen is a bee-keeper and wants to pass on this love of nature to children.

Helen works for The Alzheimer's Society as an advocate and welcomes any opportunity to raise funds for the society.

Helen Thwaites

Elizabeth Manning-Ives writes historical fiction and her third novel is due to be released soon. Elizabeth loves chocolate and insists that it stimulates and enhances her writing.

https://emiauthor76.wordpress.com/

Pam Finch

Pam Finch has written short stories, poetry and articles for publication, but it was her time of working and living in Portugal that inspired her first book, "Minho Moments" - a collection of short stories set in Northern Portugal.

Her second book, "Cappuccino Moments" are reflective and amusing tales to enjoy over a cup of coffee. Pam is currently writing her third book.

https://pamfinchwriter.wordpress.com/

Enid Thwaites

A non-fiction writer, Enid enjoys singing, gardening and painting. She is a former primary school teacher and diagnosed dyslexic. She has overcome these difficulties and has just finished writing her second book which is now being edited.

https://www.facebook.com/profile.php?id=1000091573 13072&fref=ts

Rosie Owen

Rosemarie very much enjoyed the challenge of writing a 1,000-word story for this worthwhile cause. She loves to spend time in the pool and often plans a chapter whilst swimming lengths. Her debut novel (The Tuppenny Club) will be published this year, with proceeds going to Leukaemia Research. Other favourite activities are belly dancing, yoga and spending time with her family.

Suzan Collins

Suzan writes in many styles and genres, fiction, faction and non-fiction, adults and children. She enjoys writing fiction as it allows her to make up stories to entertain readers, while eating cake, and writing non-fiction because she can share information and teach others new skills.

She is a fundraiser for the Alzheimer's Society, organising the annual Memory Walk every September with fellow author/editor Jo Wilde, and has co-authored a story book, Little Kitty, the Cat Burglar, to raise funds for Alzheimer's Research UK. This will be Suzan's second book to raise money for the charity.

To find out more about Suzan, the different pen names she uses for her writing, the writing workshops she runs and *Eafoc (raising money for Alzheimer's Research UK), or to follow her on social media, visit: www.suzancollins.com

Diana Fernando

Having been encouraged at school to keep a diary, Diana has been writing ever since, mainly articles relating to local history, letters to the papers, and some 'edgy' poems. She enjoys researching the odd and the strange. She hasn't got a novel in her - at the most a short story - as her imagination doesn't seem to stretch in that direction.

For the Millennium, she co-wrote and illustrated a book about her own North Suffolk village, and hopes to marshal her hundreds of notes for a second village book soon.

Retired from school work, Diana is still involved in teaching, via the University of the Third Age. She particularly enjoys drawing, languages and bird-watching.

Shirley Newstead

Shirley enjoyed writing her story for this anthology, and is now working on her own book, a chain of events starting with a murder. She enjoys spending time with family and friends and also loves to read whenever possible.

About the Editor

Jo Wilde

Jo was born in Yorkshire, many more years ago than she cares to remember.

She works in a theatre and a library, and fills up the rest of her time reading, writing, editing, proofreading, event organising, eating chocolate and drinking wine.

She is a fundraiser for the Alzheimer's Society, organising the annual Memory Walk every September with fellow author Suzan Collins, and has co-authored a story book, Little Kitty, the Cat Burglar, to raise funds for Alzheimer's Research UK.

To find out more about Jo and to follow her on social media, visit www.facebook.com/catberrypress

Little Kitty